Blue Skidoos to the Beach

Published by Advance Publishers, L.C.
www.advance-publishers.com

Written by Ronald Kidd
Art layout by J.J. Smith Moore
Art composition by Brad McMahon
Produced by Bumpy Slide Books

ISBN: 1-57973-081-7

Blue's Clues Discovery Series

Hi, there! Blue brought home this library book to show me what she learned about in school today.

Wow! You must have learned about the ocean, rocks, shells, and sea creatures. Cool! I love octupuses.

How about you, Blue? What's your favorite sea creature? Oh, we'll play Blue's Clues to figure it out! Yeah! Good idea!
Will you help us? You will?
Great!

Hey! Blue just skidooed into the picture! Maybe if we skidoo there, we can see some more sea creatures. Let's go! Blue skidoo, we can too!

Well, here we are! Nice beach. Whoa! There's Octopus in the water. Boy, she sure has a lot of arms to wave hello with!

Can you find any other sea creatures? Blue? She's not a sea creature! Huh? Oh, clue! Flippers are our first clue!

Okay, we're trying to figure out what Blue's favorite sea creature is, and our first clue is flippers. Hmmm . . . what do you think? Well, let's find two more clues.

Look at that cool shell Blue found! Wait a minute . . . I think it's moving!

I'm not just a shell—it's me, Hermit Crab!

Cool! A hermit crab. Hey, I like your "house"!

Wow, this is great! So far we've seen Octopus and Hermit Crab.

What's that? A clue? Where? Oh, on the beach ball. The beach ball is our second clue! So far, our clues are flippers and a beach ball. What do you think Blue's favorite sea creature is? I think we need to find our last clue.

I sure love the beach . . . the shells, the sand, the palm trees.
Oh, I almost forgot! We're looking for sea creatures. Do you see any more here?

**Good job! This beach is full of sea creatures!
There's a starfish, a sea turtle, and a lobster.**

We're back! What's that? You see a clue? On the cat? Oh, the whiskers! Whiskers are our third clue!

You know what that means, don't you? Of course! It's time to go to our . . . Thinking Chair!

So we're trying to figure out what Blue's favorite sea creature is. Our three clues are flippers, a beach ball, and whiskers. Hmmm . . .

What sea animal has flippers? That's it! A seal!
A seal has flippers, can play with a beach ball, and
has whiskers. We just figured out Blue's Clues!

Hey, Blue, I didn't know you could balance a ball on your nose! You look just like a seal! Thanks for skidooing to the beach with us and helping us solve Blue's Clues! 'Bye!

BLUE'S KEEPSAKE BEACH BOX

You will need: seashells, craft glue, a child's paintbrush, a cardboard box with lid, and crayons or markers

1. Take the lid off the box.

2. Use the paintbrush to spread a thin layer of craft glue on the lid of the box. Follow the manufacturer's directions on the glue.

3. Set the shells in the glue in any design or pattern you wish.

4. Put the box lid in a warm, dry place for the glue to dry.

5. Use crayons or markers to decorate the rest of the box.

6. Put the lid back on the box, and you have a seashell treasure box!